Ready for School, Murphy?

by Brendán Murphy

Ɗisnep · HYPERION
Los Angeles   New York

For Dad, Auntie, and Little Gran
who shaped my thoughts and dreams.
For Mam and her frogs.
And to Catherine, Aran, and Rowan
for their love and mischief.

Text and illustrations copyright © 2015 by Brendán Murphy
All rights reserved. Published by Disney·Hyperion, an imprint of Disney Book Group. No part of this book may be reproduced or transmitted in any form or by any means, electronic or mechanical, including photocopying, recording, or by any information storage and retrieval system, without written permission from the publisher. For information address Disney·Hyperion, 125 West End Avenue, New York, New York 10023.
Printed in Malaysia
First Edition, June 2015
H106-9333-5-15060
1 3 5 7 9 10 8 6 4 2

Library of Congress Cataloging-in-Publication Data

Murphy, Brendán, 1963–author, illustrator.
Ready for school, Murphy? / Brendán Murphy.—First edition.
pages cm
Summary: Murphy is full of excuses for staying home from school but his father has a cure for each of them until Murphy finally gives in—and Dad reminds him it is Saturday.
ISBN 978-1-4847-0740-1
[1. Excuses—Fiction. 2. Fathers and sons—Fiction. 3. Humorous stories.] I. Title.
PZ7.1.M87Re 2015
[E]—dc23   2014031435
Reinforced binding

Visit www.DisneyBooks.com

What's the matter, Murphy? You don't look so good.

Hmmm...
maybe I should
stay home from
school today.

...and butterflies
in my tummy.

...and butterflies
in my tummy.

Hmmm...
maybe I should
stay home from
school today.

I feel like I've got
ants in my pants...

I think it's
some kind of bug.

A bug!
We should call
the doctor. . . .

Maybe you need a shot.

Oh, that's okay. It's probably just the heebie-jeebies.

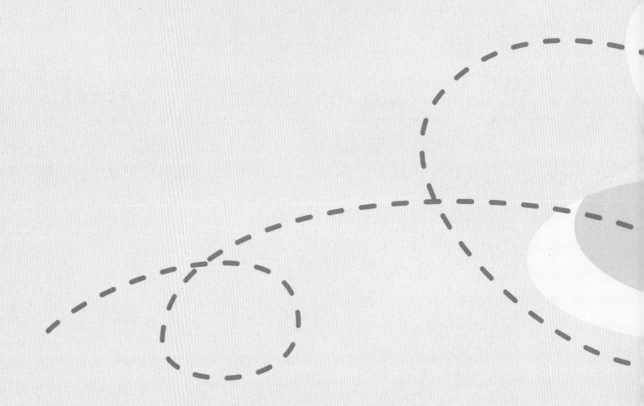

Or maybe the
goose bumps.

Then again,
it could be a
computer virus.

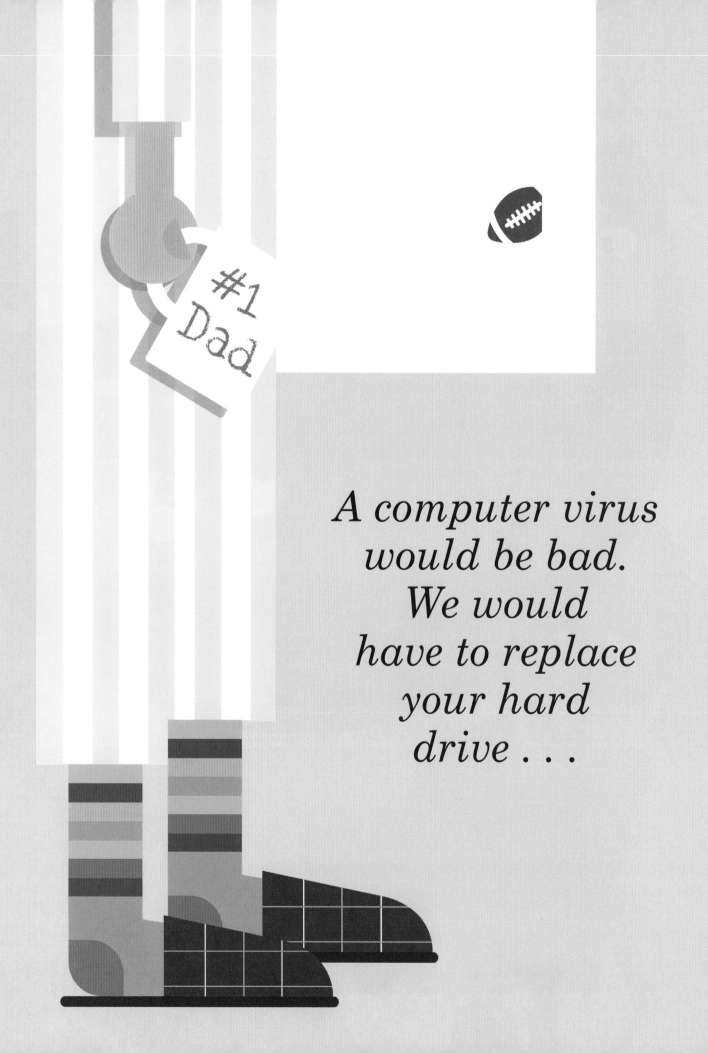

A computer virus
would be bad.
We would
have to replace
your hard
drive . . .

A computer virus
would be bad.
We would
have to replace
your hard
drive . . .

KNOCK
KNOCK

*or trade you
in for a
new model.*

or trade you in for a new model.

Teacher's desk ↓

RIBBIT

RIBBIT

No need.
I'll go get ready.

But, Murphy . . .

Yes, Dad?

It's Saturday.

Saturday?

I think
I'm feeling
better.

Gotta go!

Uh . . .
Murphy . . .

*did you forget
something?*